BEDFORDSHIRE & BUCKINGHAMSHIRE

Edited By Jenni Harrison

First published in Great Britain in 2019 by:

 Young**Writers**

Young Writers
Remus House
Coltsfoot Drive
Peterborough
PE2 9BF
Telephone: 01733 890066
Website: www.youngwriters.co.uk

FOREWORD

Welcome, Reader!

Are you ready to step back in time? Then come right this way - your time-travelling machine awaits! It's very simple, all you have to do is turn the page and you'll be transported to the past! WOW!

Is it magic? Is it a trick? No! It's all down to the skill and imagination of primary school pupils from around the country. We gave them the task of writing a story about any time in history, and to do it in just 100 words! I think you'll agree they've achieved that brilliantly – this book is jam-packed with exciting and thrilling tales from the past.

These young authors have brought history to life with their stories. This is the power of creativity and it gives us life too! Here at Young Writers we want to pass our love of the written word onto the next generation and what better way to do that than to celebrate their writing by publishing it in a book!

It sets their work free from homework books and notepads and puts it where it deserves to be – out in the world and preserved forever! Each awesome author in this book should be super proud of themselves, and now they've got proof of their imagination, their ideas and their creativity in black and white, to look back on in years to come when their first experience of publication is an ancient adventure itself!

Now I'm off to dive through the timelines and pick some winners – it's going to be difficult to choose, but I'm going to have a lot of fun along the way. I may even learn some new history facts too!

Jenni

CONTENTS

Dexter Robert Lamkin (8) 61
Isabella Grafham (8) 62
Jack Berry (8) 63
Jacob Lai (7) 64
Mitchell Whyte (8) 65
Gia Rose Patel (8) 66
Sophie Spicer (8) 67
Ella Rose Parkes (8) 68

Falconhurst School, Eaglestone

Mrithika Dhoyamoy Dhar (9) 69
Erika Plescan (8) 70
Ibraheem Chaudhry (11) 71
Madhushini Thayaparan (9) 72

Fulbrook Middle School, Woburn Sands

Ajlinka Pinder (10) 73
Sophia Blair (10) 74
Katherine Sinnott (10) 75
Aidan Harris (11) 76
Aiden Kinns (10) 77
Katie E Purdie (10) 78
Jack Edward Pearson (10) 79
Eliza Bennett (10) 80
Tora Doyle (10) 81
Hannah Kincaid (10) 82
Ollie Ditty (10) 83
Eva Cookham (10) 84
Isla Cosby-Ferguson (10) 85
Gracie Jackson-Krkoska (10) 86
Imogen Charlotte Wright (10) 87
Lily-Mae Hartley (10) 88
Ellie Bown (10) 89
Henry Kent (10) 90
Heidi Rose Yems (9) 91
Paris Connor (10) 92
Amelia Nicholls (10) 93

Thomas Longstaffe (10) 94
Millie Wardley (10) 95
Alejandro López (9) 96
Jake Bradshaw 97
Alexander Lee (10) 98

Priory Primary School, Greyfriars

Jabir 99
Moaaz Mostafa 100
Negmeldin (10)

Putnoe Primary School, Bedford

Wahid Choudhury (10) 101
Abigail Winn (10) 102
Shanay Francois (9) 103
Numa Nazahah (10) 104
Arjun Sikand (10) 105
Daniella Adjei-Asante (10) 106
Alyssia Brown (10) 107
Karan Mahey (9) 108
Alexander Buczkowski (10) 109
Gabriela Stryjewska (11) 110
Delia Florentina Crimu (9) 111
Archie Schaffer (10) 112
Scarlett Smith (10) 113
Leana Tihomirova (9) 114
Alaia Elizabeth Walton- 115
Kale (11)
Georgia Coblenz (9) 116
George Mhitaryan (10) 117
Ibrahim Ali Hussain (10) 118
Michael Oliver (10) 119
Dane Robertshaw (10) 120
Isabelle Smith (9) 121
Amelia Kulik (10) 122
Faith Flawn (10) 123
Niamh Bailey (10) 124
Jack Garratt (9) 125

Jessica Jayne Hawkins (10)   126

Sharnbrook Primary School, Sharnbrook

Ethan Andrew Rushton (8)   127
Ezequiel Cutting (9)   128
Storm Chambers (8)   129
Harrison Michael Welch (9)   130
Jessica Steele (9)   131
Eloise Hope Cannon (9)   132
Ava Howard (9)   133

St Mary's RC Primary School, Caddington

Darren Kunaishe   134
Machingauta (11)
Ashley Claude Sheila   135
Davies (11)
Rosie Ellis-Emery (11)   136
Emma Lawrence (11)   137
Michal Antoniuk (11)   138
Sonny Bateman (10)   139
Ronnie-Mae Begley (11)   140
Gabriel Darling (10)   141

The Linden Academy, Luton

Irisz Ubierbor King (8)   142
Emily Grace Phinn (8)   143
Jonathan Kwaku Henaku   144
Ansah (8)
Ume-Laila Kazmi   145
Amerie Njawaya (8)   146
Lilie Rosie Gray (8)   147

Whitehouse Primary School, Whitehouse

Jin Saleyi (11)   148
Francesca Charalambous (12)   149
Shubh Suman (10)   150
Loyin Assan (11)   151
Hayden Woodall (11)   152
Aathmika Kiritharan (11)   153
Marta Monteiro (11)   154
Jai Nathwani (11)   155
Aadil Khota (11)   156

THE
MINI SAGAS

Heaven Or Hell

I woke up. Nothing was the same. Moments ago, my death had overcome my living soul. The death of a pharaoh. Choosing my steps strategically, trying not to fail my true destiny. Walking forward, my only path. I stumbled across light. Light and darkness (commonly known as heaven and hell). I had found my next path; my life was complete.

"No, your door is that one!" bellowed and old, gruelling voice.

"Yep, hell it is!" spoke a second.

"No, no!" I screeched.

"Sorry sir, no can do!" cried the first voice. Out of my anger and rage, I sieged on.

Archie Richardson (10)
Aston Clinton School, Aston Clinton

Silenced

It was a perfect day. The birds hummed playfully as feet hit the dusty path like raindrops. That's when my life changed. Two soldiers were leaning in the doorway. "Hello, can I be of assistance?"
"Due to your husband's death, you will be stripped of your wealth. If you want to see your family again, you will fight in the Colosseum."
Before I could sputter a word, they seized my arms and dragged me through the dirt. Villagers laughed at me bitterly, throwing fruit at my filthy face.
I looked through the bars, drowning in dread. I had to win.

Thomas Kemp (10)
Aston Clinton School, Aston Clinton

The Roman Rabbit

"There's no hope," sobbed Sniffius. "We're on our sixth race and we haven't won yet!"
"Get out there!" yelled Marcus. "All of you."
A team of five who were Sniffius the pilot and the four runners Caius, Cadmus, Cato and Cyrus. The race started with the call of a horn. They were off. Team Rabbit were off to a good start taking third place. As Team Rabbit made their way around, they took second place and then first. Behind them was Team Ferret who were in trouble and about to die. But then Sniffius turned and saved them!

Riley McMahon (10)
Aston Clinton School, Aston Clinton

An Egyptian Reality?

Izzy was just a normal girl, playing outside with her ball. As she bounced it up and down, a dark mist suddenly swirled around her. Izzy felt scared whilst it was transforming into a ghost. It was the ghost of Egypt. "Take my hand," it whispered, as the mysterious ghost stamped her with the mark of Anubis. Anubis, the Egyptian god of death appeared. Izzy ran for her life. Thinking about all her family at home, tears filled her eyes.
"Jack, time for tea," called Mum.
Jack turned his computer simulator off and Izzy felt the world shrinking around her.

Izzy Lawson (10)
Aston Clinton School, Aston Clinton

The Attack

Brutus stumbled out of the wooden boat, which had carried him to England. He was frightened because this was his first real Roman mission and he had only ever trained with wooden swords. Instantly, he started work, laying down stones to make a road. Later, a group of half-naked men, covered in warpaint, leapt out of the bushes beside him. Immediately, they started attacking the Romans with their double-handed swords and axes. Brutus grabbed his shortsword and aided his comrades in battle. All of a sudden, he felt a blow to his temple. Everything slowly faded away...

Duncan Oglesby (10)
Aston Clinton School, Aston Clinton

Time Travelers And The Mysteries Of Time

Two friends called Jess and Jack built a time machine. They named it Time Blast. They both got in and started it. They ended up in the Jurassic period. As it stopped, they fell asleep.

Roar! The sound woke Jack and Jess up. "Run!" Jess shouted. They ran further than ever. Jack found a log to hide. Suddenly, an ankylosaurus broke the log and chased after them. They lost it, then a T-rex spotted them. All of a sudden, all the dinosaurs fell asleep and so did they.

Ten hours later they woke up. A dinosaur was carrying them...

William Pearson
Aston Clinton School, Aston Clinton

The Trip To The Moon

Three, two, one, blast off! They had finally started their journey to space. Everyone on board the shiny spaceship was very excited. In the distance, Earth was getting smaller and smaller as they went further into the galaxy. Out of the window, they could see huge meteors coming past the spaceship. They really hoped they wouldn't get hit by one of the huge meteors. Out of the front window, they could see the moon. Excitement filled the spaceship. It got closer and closer and before they knew it, with a crash they'd finally landed safely.

Taylah Rice (10)
Aston Clinton School, Aston Clinton

The Cat Of The Night

It was midnight in the street. The Black Death I am blamed for roamed it, making me feel nauseous. Suddenly, the pounding of feet commenced. I was off, darting into a road, the man sprinting behind. My charcoal coat was the shadows, my ivory socks the dappled glow of a streetlamp. Suddenly, a well loomed in front of me. My head crashed into it and I fell. The man towered above me, wielding a dagger, a wicked grin contorting his face.
Here I am now, lost and defenceless. The dagger swipes down for the final kiss. Will I see tomorrow...?

Rose Pillai (10)
Aston Clinton School, Aston Clinton

The Roman Invasion

Crash... clang... crash... The noise of heavy pieces of metal hitting each other filled the air. I was a young Celtic farmer and the noise of this frightened me. What was it? I found the answer to my question moments later. Marching up and over the hill was a whole army of Roman soldiers! Leading them was a tall, strong-looking man - their general. Within seconds, we had picked up our swords and were charging towards our enemies. Although I knew I was only a child, I could still have a chance. Would it be enough to beat the Romans?

Eloise Geary (10)
Aston Clinton School, Aston Clinton

The Victorian Street Child Struggling For Life!

Once I grabbed the loaf of bread, all I could do was run. I slipped down the alleyway. My stomach was empty. I was surprised I had the energy to run. Quickly and stealthily, I snuck through the gap in the fence where all the other street urchins were sleeping. I could hear traders shouting, children crying, men working. I divided the bread for the ten of us. The mouthwatering food gave me a warm feeling as it travelled down my throat. This was all I might eat today. I shouted to my fellow urchins, "Let's go pick some pockets!"

Safia Alqassar (9)
Aston Clinton School, Aston Clinton

My Gladiator Adventure!

The most terrifying moment of my life was, unfortunately, here in the Colosseum. I stepped out the gloomy dungeons into the sandy pit. The sound of the crowd screaming was deafening. The gate at the other end started to open. My heart pounded. As my opponent rushed towards me, I raised my sword high in the air. He was the size of two men put together, twice my size. I was too frightened so I shouted, "I surrender!" The crowd fell silent. I thought they took it well until they started booing. Should I run away or stay and fight?

Holly Merrin (10)
Aston Clinton School, Aston Clinton

The Shadow

As I roamed the woods I saw it; the thing I'd travelled miles for. A gleaming sword made of pure platinum. A sword once held by the god Zeus. A sword that fought in- "Roar!" came a noise from behind the bramble bush. After its blood-curdling scream came its shadow, a heart-taking shadow. I ran and ran, but it was too quick. It jumped from branch to branch, gaining momentum from each and every step. "Argh!" I screamed, hoping I had lost it. I saw the flag for my camp. When I looked back I saw... it was a squirrel!

Harrison Rolfe (10)
Aston Clinton School, Aston Clinton

Fear Not

I'm here under the floorboards, hungry, just waiting for some crumbs to fall. I have to be careful. Humans have always been scared of me, I think it's my tail and the way I scurry around they don't like, but at the minute they're terrified. Everyone has a cat to try to kill me. I have no idea why. It's funny really, they should be afraid of that sneezing noise they make because after that they start to vomit and their skin turns black then they just vanish. For good. That would definitely scare me if I was a human.

Kayleigh Cornhill (10)
Aston Clinton School, Aston Clinton

This Was The Day That Changed My Life Forever

I couldn't believe there was this much blood. I was putting my armour on when another gladiator walked back from the arena with blood pouring down the side of his face. I wasn't sure if it was his or his opponents. The more blood I saw, the more scared I became.

It was my turn to face the horror. I stepped out. A few seconds later the horn blew; the battle commenced. I tried to slice my sword through his armour but it was too thick. The last thing I remembered was my opponent grabbing a dagger, aiming and throwing...

Mira Lowenna Daddow (10)
Aston Clinton School, Aston Clinton

14

What Happened To Boudicca?

It was too late. The Romans had won. Boudicca had to save the Iceni tribe. It was time to run! The tribe were dropping like flies. Boudicca stumbled into a blackberry bush. She felt a sudden tap on her shoulder. Was it a Roman? Not Roman but another tribe, who might be able to help! Boudicca assumed a new look and identity. She soon settled into a new life as a jewellery maker. Fast forward 1958 years. A young girl playing suddenly tripped. She had found a box of unusual jewellery. Each piece was marked 'Bou'.

Freya May Cattermole (10)
Aston Clinton School, Aston Clinton

Attack!

It was a dark, eerie night. I was hiding behind a tree when suddenly... "Jump! Attack!" shouted a scary voice. I knew exactly who it was. It was Brad's (my best friend) mum. Brad's mum was the queen of our tribe. We were at war! I ran into battle thinking I was ready, I was not. The leader of the enemy was Python and I was attacking him. Me, a skinny thirteen-year-old against the leader. I was no match. He pinned me down, there was nothing I could do. He slowly applied pressure to my weak, soft neck...

Clara Michael (10)
Aston Clinton School, Aston Clinton

A Matter Of Life And Death

The malevolent, amber sun was just bleeding through the shades of dawn as I would be soon. The nightmare of shattering to pieces at a lion's roar still haunts me. The bars of my unilluminated cell took me back to many moons ago, when my answers had turned into questions. But all I remembered was coming and going, a beginning and end. Time waits for no man, they used to say. How right they were. The gate of fate slowly uncovered a killing zone. The arena looked blurry through my bloody eye, but I knew I was there.

Alyce Megan Aird (10)
Aston Clinton School, Aston Clinton

Mummy Madness!

I emerged from the shadows and crawled into a mountain of riches. Beside me, canopic jars stood to attention as they guarded the pharaoh and his tomb. Like a jaguar prowling through the jungle, I explored the beauty around me. Suddenly, a loud grumble from the tomb pierced through the air and the box burst open. Out stepped the mummy. Snow-white linen was wrapped all around him and beady, coal-black eyes dug into my skin. I screamed, the sound echoing off the walls and watched in horror. It was charging at me...

Lily-Rose Greville (10)
Aston Clinton School, Aston Clinton

The Battle

Death was not an option as I ran chopping and slicing by Boudicca's side. The battle had begun. I ran and swung my sword. *Chop!* A man's head flew to the floor. One dropped to his knees and prayed. Suddenly, I had a sudden feeling of guilt until I was knocked unconscious.

When I woke I seemed to be in line for the chop. Man after man after man. The blade was red. I felt a sudden movement in my pocket. It was a dagger. Finally it was my turn and I stabbed the man!

Hayden Carey (10)
Aston Clinton School, Aston Clinton

A Night Of Terror!

She was trapped in the pyramid. Trapped with only the dead body that had died over 1000 years ago. Matilda was a ten-year-old girl who had been sent to the Egyptians by an evil wizard. She had ended up in the tomb of a dead Egyptian. All she could see was the faint outline of the sarcophagus. She could hear nothing but her own breath and could smell the mustiness of the dead body.
Suddenly, a figure sat up from the sarcophagus. The mummy was coming towards her...!

Willow Wiseman (10)
Aston Clinton School, Aston Clinton

The Blitz

We heard the siren warning us that it was time to run! The bombs were coming soon. Mum grabbed my hand and I followed close behind. We had to get to the underground, fast. Once we found our beds we could hear the bombs above us like a giant coming after you.

We realised that we forgot our food to survive. I sat on the dusty bed thinking about my dad fighting in the war.

The city went quiet, nobody knew if it was safe...

Isla Cruse (10)
Aston Clinton School, Aston Clinton

The Volcano

Drusus looked up. Why build a city so near a volcano? According to the rich, it would never erupt.
Meanwhile, Hortensia watched down from the window onto the busy Roman roads. It was still early morning and the city was still awaking, even though it didn't seem so. There was a noise... a crackle... no human could create it so it must be... the volcano! "Run! Flee!" a lady shouted. Was anyone safe?

Lucy Akehurst (10)
Aston Clinton School, Aston Clinton

Trapped

The warm sun burned my face as I stopped in my tracks. I stared up at the wide entrance. Did I dare go inside the tall, golden structures? I raced in past the entrance and through the dark tunnels. Stood in front of me was an ancient pharaoh's tomb. Carefully, I edged closer. A bony fist crept out the side of the tomb. Without a second thought, I turned to run away. I couldn't get out. I had awoken the dead!

Leah Williams (9)
Aston Clinton School, Aston Clinton

The Chimney

I stood there, my heart pounding in my chest. I could hear the voice of my master urging me up the chimney. I stepped in. My whole world went black. I started to climb up the ashy bricks. Suddenly, a wisp of wind pushed past me and made me lose my balance. I had fallen. I kept falling and falling, wondering what my world would be like once I had hit the ground. *Thud!* I was knocked out cold...

Faith Trustram (10)
Aston Clinton School, Aston Clinton

The Fight Of The Ages

It was early 68BC as I fought Spartacus in the Colosseum, hoping to win my victory and to be able to go back home. The crowds were cheering as Spartacus slashed his sword down my cheek. As he cut my cheek I managed to knock his sword out of his hand and use my shield to knock him over. The crowds cheered for me as I won. The fight had been my victory and I was able to return to my family.

Frankie Murphy (10)
Aston Clinton School, Aston Clinton

Raging Romans

Once, when the Roman army were doing their duties they ran into Boudicca. "Charge!" said the leader.

"Yes sir!" said one troop.

"Yes," blabbered all the others and kept on blabbering.

"Charge!" demanded the Emperor. "Come on, less blabbering more... you know... stabbing. Chop chop!"

"Okay, fine," said one troop.

"Very well," said the rest, and so they started attacking.

A few days later, they finished, well they thought they were. Then a troop saw Boudicca running to a shed. Boudicca attempted to poison herself and she succeeded.

"We won!" they shouted.

Jake Clegg (8)
Burford School, Marlow Bottom

Release The Rhino

It was 80AD in Rome. The crowd cheered loudly as the gladiators ran into the Colosseum. Emperor Titus yelled, "Release the beast!" Snorting and charging, the rhino stormed into the arena like a fierce bull. Emperor Titus commanded, "Gladiators, fight!"
The gladiators drew their swords and held up their shields. The rhino charged at them and dented Spartacus's shield. The crowd booed.
Suddenly, Marcus turned around and ordered, "Stop!" He realised this was the rhino he'd saved from ivory hunters in Africa. The crowd fell silent. The rhino stood as still as a statue... then licked Marcus's face.

Luke Holmes-Garrad (8)
Burford School, Marlow Bottom

Rome Is Burning

The air was scorching. Rome was burning. Nero sat in his chair watching Rome burn whilst playing the fiddle.

"I curse you Nero for being a ridiculous man!" cried Jupiter. The fire got worse. Italy was down to ash and people lay dead, burnt to a crisp.

"Should I have helped Rome?" queried Nero.

"Of course! Yes!" exclaimed Jupiter.

"My precious wine! It's gone! Wine!" Nero cried out, sobbing.

Four years passed. Nero had enough - he could take no more of his burning guilt and he pleaded someone to end his misery. His final words were... "Too late!"

William Kinder (8)
Burford School, Marlow Bottom

The Romans Who Live Under My Bed

I jumped up into bed and pulled up the covers.
"Goodnight Zac," said Mum. "Sweet dreams."
Bam! Crash! Smash! We were under attack.
"Argh!" The Romans were under my bed! Suddenly a Roman soldier released my fish from their tank into the sea surrounding my bed. Next, they marched two by two and started a water fight.
"Help! They are destroying my room!" I reached for my Nerf gun and fired all of the Romans out of my window.
"Mum, did you see the Romans under my bed last night?" I asked.
"It was all a dream!" Mum said.

Zachary Gibson (8)
Burford School, Marlow Bottom

The Faraway Adventures Of The Time Lapse Cave

A long time ago in Egypt lived two best friends, Miranda Nikelwood and Noah Arch. Miranda, Noah and Icicle the husky dog found a cave west of the tombs leading them into different time periods, and this is where their story begins.

One day, they set off and stepped into their beloved cave. Suddenly, Miranda felt tension in the air as it felt like someone was following them.

"Noah, I think someone's following us."

"Oh, don't be silly Mindy," bellowed Noah, but a figure lurked in the shadows as they turned on their heel. Who could this mysterious person be?

Charlotte Mellor (8)
Burford School, Marlow Bottom

The Final Fight

Suddenly, Bonecrusher Barry entered the arena. Everyone gasped at his gigantic, muscular form. The other gladiators stared in horror and I honestly thought they might faint. Bonecrusher slowly drew his bloodstained mace as he walked towards them with explosive steps. Gladiator Gordon and Indefeaticus trembled before Bonecrusher and they were paralysed in fear. He began to swing his mace with destructive power, faster and faster it went. It flew out of his hand like lightning and smashed the gladiators into the wall. They never lived to tell the tale. Indefeaticus was finally defeated.

Joshua Urie (8)
Burford School, Marlow Bottom

The Girl In Rome!

When Lilla was in class, they were learning about a new topic. The topic was the Romans and Lilla had a late night so she was tired and she said, "I am very tired Miss!" When they were watching a video she fell asleep!

She dreamt that she was travelling through time and when she awoke she was in Rome and she was wearing a tunic. Lilla said, "Where am I?"

A weird, strange person came up to her and said, "What's your name?"

Lilla said, "Lilla Hogwarts."

The stranger took her to a sign that said 'Rome 973BC'...

Millie Gray (8)
Burford School, Marlow Bottom

Roman Life

The Romans came to Britain nearly 2000 years ago and changed our country. Even today, evidence of the Romans can be seen in the ruins of Roman buildings, forts, roads and baths can be found all over Britain. For example, they gave us underfloor heating, concrete, straight roads and aqueducts. In case you didn't know, the Romans lived in Rome which is in the middle of Italy. The Romans didn't just invade Britain, they invaded other countries too. The Romans invaded Europe, North Africa and the Middle East. The ancient Romans worshipped a lot of different gods and goddesses.

Mia Jessica Morton (7)
Burford School, Marlow Bottom

Chaser's Day Out

One sunny day, Chaser the Viking decided to fly across the ocean on his dragon and look out for treasure. He found something he had never seen before. It was an aeroplane. Chaser sat inside it but realised he couldn't fly it. People living on the island saw Chaser trying to fly their plane and screamed, "Vikings! Vikings!" Chaser got petrified and flew up on his dragon but was soon followed by islanders on their plane. Suddenly, the plane ran out of fuel and crashed. Chaser said, "Phew! My dragon is better than theirs!" And vowed he'd steal no more.

Riya Rawat (8)
Burford School, Marlow Bottom

The Time Machine

Once there was a girl who built a time machine!
She landed in Roman Britain. Within seconds she
spotted a frightening group of fierce soldiers
striding towards her. However, there was a wild-
looking woman with red hair fighting back against
the terrifying group. She spotted the scared little girl
and commanded, "Get into my chariot child. My
name is Boudicca, Queen of the Iceni tribe. I am
trying to get my land back from the Roman
invaders." Boudicca gave her an incredible choice.
"Would you like to join my army or go back to
where you belong, brave girl?"

Ella Wiggs Steele (8)
Burford School, Marlow Bottom

Close Encounter

Propellers spinning, engine screaming, I took off into the clear blue sky. Over the English Channel, a small dot appeared dead ahead, coming closer by the second. Frightened, I dove under and swooped up behind it to get a closer look. It was a Messerschmidt. I opened fire and shot through the wings and body. The plane started smoking and nose-dived downwards. Whilst I was enjoying victory, my plane started juddering. As I plummeted down towards the dark beaches of Normandy, I pulled open the cockpit window and bailed out to find myself in the hands of a surprised Frenchman.

Benjamin Richards (8)
Burford School, Marlow Bottom

Florence Nightingale Deals With Blood

Many years ago, there lived an amazingly caring Italian lady called Florence Nightingale. As the Crimean War was going on, and as the closest hospital had terribly poor conditions with disgusting germs, she decided to go and lend a hand. It was a frightening job for poor Florence as she dealt with extremely wounded soldiers. Blood spurted everywhere, as a soldier came in with missing arms and legs. Florence was so caring to the injured soldiers that she was named the Lady with the Lamp. It was really hard at times, however, Florence always persevered and never gave up.

Jemima Jane Hillier (8)
Burford School, Marlow Bottom

Mighty Mount Vesuvius

Once upon a time, there was a beautiful city called Pompeii in Italy. It was a calm, sunny morning and without any warning, Vesuvius erupted. Magma shot out and blasted everywhere. It sounded like a nuclear bomb going off. People were screaming and running for their lives. They thought that the end of the world had begun. A pyroclastic surge tumbled through the streets, covering everybody in grey, smouldering ash. All the scared, hopeless people turned into terrifying statues. This eruption turned out to be one of the worst volcanic eruptions in history.

Jack O'Reilly (7)
Burford School, Marlow Bottom

Gladiator

When the mighty warrior Vincenzo entered the Colosseum, the crowd cheered wildly for him as the other gladiators followed. Lions and tigers were waiting for them. The battle began, people were charging at each other so Vincenzo went for a lion. It was terrifying. Nearly every minute, someone was injured or dead or eaten. When two gladiators are left and one is on the ground, the emperor puts his thumb down and the gladiator dies, or if up, he survives. The emperor put his thumb up! Vincenzo had earned his freedom and he went to Africa to forget his past.

Vincent Proffitt (8)
Burford School, Marlow Bottom

Day At The Colosseum

My ancient adventure is set in the heart of Rome in AD79 and is about best friends called Fabia and Pax who went to the Colosseum to see gladiators fight. When they got there they found their seats and were feeling a bit nervous and excited. What a show it was! There was fighting, screeching, and lots and lots of cheering from the crowd. The Colosseum was very hot and loud and the gladiators looked tired and were injured. After the frightful show, Pax and Fabia left the Colosseum to go home. The day was very shocking, thrilling and horrible.

Grace Suder (8)
Burford School, Marlow Bottom

The Great Trek

Back in 1835, SA faced a great divide. The Dutch, who couldn't stand the Brits, gathered up their precious bits. They set off on an endless trek, prepared for somewhat of a schlep. Horses, oxen, wagons. They travelled on for many weeks, crossing rivers, climbing peaks. Forced to save their group of cattle, they were often forced to battle. After fighting many wars, they were free to make their laws.
A lesson here for all to see, we all have an identity. And while we hope the world unites, when some see wrong, others... right.

Eva Martin (8)
Burford School, Marlow Bottom

The Dino Chase

Once there was a boy called Josh and he lost his father called Robert. Josh couldn't find Robert and he thought that he was in the forest so he ran into the forest. Josh was scared because the sun was setting and a T-rex found Josh, so Josh ran. He found someone called James and he was a dino hunter. James said, "Run!" so they did.
James found a way out so they ran towards it. Once they were out, they found Robert and he said, "Thank you for keeping my son safe."
They lived happily ever after.

Josh Bundock (8)
Burford School, Marlow Bottom

Terrified

I was fed up. Dad had gone hunting, Mum was picking berries and I was looking after Delilah. Suddenly, a loud roar came from the bushes and before I could blink, a huge cave bear had pounced on Delilah and was pulling her into the bushes. I had to save her. No time to get a spear, I grabbed a branch and set it alight in the campfire. Screaming, I threw the burning branch at the bear. He was terrified, letting Delilah go before running away. Delilah stopped crying and said, "Thank you best brother. You saved me."

Dylan Sexton (7)
Burford School, Marlow Bottom

YoungWriters

The Nepalese Earthquake

On a hot sunny morning, everyone was doing
normal things like buying bread or playing or
cooking. I was reading under a shady tree with my
friends Arthur, Peter and Liam. In the blink of an
eye, tremors started to happen. We all felt calm
because there were always tremors in Nepal.
Suddenly, an enormous earthquake struck. I felt
scared, nervous, even petrified. I had no idea what
to do so I ran as fast as I could run. Luckily, we
took shelter and survived. All of our parents died so
we took care of each other and lived.

Josh Thaliwal (8)
Burford School, Marlow Bottom

The Pyramid

The pyramid was like a maze with twists and turns everywhere. Jack and I were looking at marks on the wall. When we turned around the tour guide had disappeared! We were all alone in the dark, gloomy passage. We ran into a large chamber. In front of us was a coffin decorated with gold and jewels. We realised the door was slightly ajar. We heard a low groaning noise behind us. We turned slowly and came face-to-face with a figure dressed in dirty white bandages. The figure moved slowly towards us. We were trapped.......

Brody Wilson (8)
Burford School, Marlow Bottom

The Ugly Roman

Once upon a time, around 2000 years ago, an ugly baby was born. This baby was not like any other child in Pompeii. Everyone smirked, giggled and even bullied him. One time, on Romans Got Talent, people threw tomatoes at him when he walked on stage!
But, one day, at 3.33pm, an odd wizard appeared right in front of him. His family gasped, "Argh!" The wizard came and turned him into a handsome and strong young man. He entered himself into the war and won for the Romans of Pompeii. Everyone now loved him.

Holly Dennison (8)
Burford School, Marlow Bottom

Big Bird In The Sky

It was a beautiful day. We went to a lake in the south of France. I was having so much fun swimming with my mummy. Suddenly I looked up in the sky and saw a huge bird. It looked like a plane. I yelled, "Big bird! Big bird!"
My mummy replied, "It's a pterodactyl!"
I couldn't believe it! I had never seen one before. It had very large wings and flew super fast. I ran out of the water to take a picture to show my friends but it was gone. I feel lucky that I have seen a pterodactyl.

Kieron Walls (8)
Burford School, Marlow Bottom

An Adventure Of A Roman Daughter

In ancient times, a girl called Bobbie lived in Rome. Her father was a soldier in the Roman army. One day, her father had to go to war in Britannia. Bobbie was very worried. She wanted to see her father fight so she decided to travel in secret on a cart, hidden in a sack of straw.

Whilst travelling through a forest she met a Barbarian girl who was the same age as her. When they arrived at the battlefield they were horrified by the destruction that they saw, so the two girls decided they would stop the war...

Scarlett Speare (8)
Burford School, Marlow Bottom

The Gladiator

Once upon a time, there was a boy called Remus and he wanted to be a famous gladiator. He grew up at a gladiator academy and trained for matches. When he was older he became a gladiator and won most battles. Today was an important battle because if he won he would be a free man!
The battle started and the crowd cheered. Remus struck his trident at the other competitor, knocking him to the ground. Remus had won! He was then a free man and famous for what he'd done. He then carried on living a normal life.

Isaac Pack (8)
Burford School, Marlow Bottom

The Mighty Mount Vesuvius

In a faraway land at the top of a mountain was a very powerful volcano, it was named Mount Vesuvius. Mount Vesuvius was very mighty indeed. Under Mount Vesuvius was a little town called Pompeii. It was full of people. They believed that Mount Vesuvius gave them luck each day. But one day, Mount Vesuvius did something bad that the people of Pompeii didn't know would happen. It erupted. It rumbled and destroyed everything. It also caused a big tsunami. Lots of people tried to run away. Sadly, most people died.

Phoebe L-R (7)
Burford School, Marlow Bottom

The Mummy Revenge

Once in ancient Egypt, there was a chef who worked for the king. The king liked posh food but the chef made horrible food. He made sheep's head with ice cream. Yuck! The king got so tired of the disgusting food he threw him in the dungeon. The chef cried and cried but realised there was lots of toilet roll. He wrapped himself up like a mummy. He broke through the wall and escaped. He went to all the shops in the kingdom to scare everyone away to get his revenge on the king. He lived happily ever after.

Eloise Hughes (8)
Burford School, Marlow Bottom

Boudicca's Magic

Boudicca looked around her wealthy kingdom bravely. She wasn't scared that the Romans were coming because she had a strong army. Boudicca decided to go for a quiet walk in the peaceful forest before the evil Roman army reached her. When she got to the middle of the eerie forest she saw a small oak door so she went inside and heard someone. She was going to kill it with her sword but her sword had turned into a sparkling magical wand. She knew what she would do now, she would turn the Romans into ugly frogs!

Florrie Marsh (8)
Burford School, Marlow Bottom

The Gladiator's Freedom

There was a man living a normal life, when out of the mist sailed a Roman ship. The slave-dealer forced him on board. He was sent for food at the market until someone bought him. He called that person 'Master'. His master sent him to be a gladiator and he was good at it because he won battle after battle, competing in many coliseums where he turned into the best of the best. Finally, he made it to the amphitheatre. The Emperor put in a man called Calisius who lost. The crowd gave the man a name - Felix.

Felix Gregan (8)
Burford School, Marlow Bottom

Antonius And The Wolf

Breathless. There was a silence where all I could hear was the drumming of my heart beating. Then, I sprinted for my life through all of the moist, elegant trees. There was a furry, scruffy creature reaching for me as if I was its prey. It was trying to grab me but I was too fast. Suddenly, pulling hard, the dark, disguised creature dropped onto me. Glaring, its beady eyes stared at me. Then I knew exactly what it was. "Wolf! Argh!" I screamed. I thought I would never see the light of day ever again.

Poppy Regan (8)
Burford School, Marlow Bottom

Mummy Madness

The wind whistled as I approached a tomb and sand was flying everywhere. Suddenly. there was a banging sound coming from inside the tomb. Then I could just make out something or someone was coming towards me and it was walking like a zombie. I froze on the spot. It started to run at me so I quickly ran away. My heart was pounding in my chest. Its hands grabbed me so I screamed and turned around. I was staring into its dark eyes and then I realised that it was covered fully in white bandages. It was a mummy...

Sophie Rose Squire (8)
Burford School, Marlow Bottom

The Hero Of Pompeii!

It was a normal day and Cato was on holiday in Pompeii. The streets were bustling with people all going to the market as normal, but the next day everyone was heading to the harbour. Some people suspected that nothing was happening, but Cato knew what to do. He knocked on every door and smashed every letterbox to spread the news about Mount Vesuvius erupting. Everyone ran as fast as they could to escape the volcano. Cato found a lost girl so he led her to the harbour. Everyone was safe apart from Cato...

Isobel Butler (8)
Burford School, Marlow Bottom

Attack Of The Romans

It was a sunny day and I was scavenging for food. I heard a loud stamping sound and I trembled in fear. In the distance, I saw an army of Romans waving sharp swords running towards me. I managed to hide where I thought they wouldn't find me. Families were being killed all around me. Suddenly, I felt someone behind me. I looked back and I saw a sword coming towards me. I felt a sharp pain and I fell to the ground. Luckily, he moved on to the next victim as I played dead. I'd survived another day.

Jasper Lai (7)
Burford School, Marlow Bottom

The Gladiators

Once there were two slaves. They were friends. They went to a ludi, but one went to the ludi which only trained slaves to be hoplomachus and the other one a cestus. Learning to fight was extremely challenging. They went to fight in the spectacular Colosseum. But when they got there they realised they were against each other, so they didn't do very well at entertaining so the crowd booed. One of them chopped the other's head off. The crowd cheered and the Emperor came down and congratulated him.

Finley Harvey (8)
Burford School, Marlow Bottom

The Cave

One evening, Bob, Jeff and Fred went out to catch animals for their dinner. In the distance, they saw a cave but it wasn't an ordinary one, it had pictures of animals on the cave. Bob, Jeff and Fred walked over to the cave. Bob was thinking there were animals in the cave because there were animals drawn on the cave but he might be wrong. As they reached the cave, Bob had a little look in the cave to see if it was safe. Luckily it was safe, it was just people doing drawings on the wall with flint.

Alessandra Jedras (8)
Burford School, Marlow Bottom

The Eruption

Within the bustling city of Pompeii, Marcus sat eating a scrap of bread he had found in a dark corner of an alleyway. Suddenly, he felt the ground shake and the sky turned as black as soot. Marcus looked up to the mighty mountain that stood before him. Glowing, yellow liquid dripped down the sides like treacle. A hot, bubbling substance shot out of the mouth of the mountain like an array of bright explosions. Every bone in Marcus' body was filled with fear. He knew he had to run. Run fast.

Jack Morgan (8)
Burford School, Marlow Bottom

The Chase

Tom fiddled at his watch, thinking it wasn't working. As he looked up he was there, the Jurassic. He fell over he noticed the dinosaur eggs, he carefully put them in his explorer bag. Tom walked into a lake. Nothing was there. He started drinking and then a spinosaurus came! He ran out of the water as fast as he could. The wind howled. He spun his watch, moving to the Triassic, then to the Stone Age and then straight to 2019. Then he felt his back shake. The dinosaur egg had hatched...

Dexter Robert Lamkin (8)
Burford School, Marlow Bottom

Stone Age Monster

The wind howled, we carried spears and the gloomy moon led the way through the forest. The trees rustled and one tree fell down and we heard a frightful scream. We looked away from whatever was there, but whatever it was was harmful. Suddenly, I turned back and my friends had disappeared. I turned back again and the moonlight shone on the beast. It had sharp, white teeth, blood-red jaws and sharp, pointy claws like a needle and thread. The moon was too bright. It turned. It was a bear...

Isabella Grafham (8)
Burford School, Marlow Bottom

Boudicca Revolts The Romans

One day, I tried to look out across the horizon, but pitch-black smoke covered everything as far as I could see. Disaster had struck, Londinium was ablaze. My jaw dropped open, I could not believe my eyes. The stories I had heard about Boudicca, the warrior queen, leading a revolt against the Romans were all coming to life! She had destroyed the city that I had loved. Feeling shocked and scared, I watched Londinium burn to a pile of ashes. I knew that life would never be the same again.

Jack Berry (8)
Burford School, Marlow Bottom

The Vikings

In ancient Norway. there was a powerful Viking called Fred. One day. he was on a longship ready to invade Britain. He got his army and got ready to fight. A few minutes later, they landed on an island in Britain. I found two Vikings with tattered armour. I told Fred and he rescued them. Their names were Sam and Jack so we gave them some new armour and we took them to battle. Many soldiers were killed but I survived and so did Fred, Sam and Jack. Over 2000 soldiers were killed.

Jacob Lai (7)
Burford School, Marlow Bottom

Pharaoh Big Nose And The Half-Dead Man

A long, long time ago lived a very very rich pharaoh whos name was Pharaoh Big Nose. One day, he decided to make an underground pyramid. Then one of the miners said, "What's that?" It was a mummy! Everyone ran out of the mine. Then the pharaoh decided to see it. When he saw the mummy, it got up and started chasing the pharaoh. Then all of the mummies awoke so he ran out of the mine and said to all of his men to kill them all, which they did in two seconds flat!

Mitchell Whyte (8)
Burford School, Marlow Bottom

The Shadow Behind

I was exploring in a snowy wood when a shadow
approached me. I could feel a warm breath on my
neck and my hairs stood up. I could smell blood
mixed with snowy mountain air and I ran as fast as
I could. Then I heard a roaring noise behind me
and I was petrified. I came to a halt in front of a cliff
edge. It felt as if my heart rose to my throat and I
had tingly legs. I could hear the pounding of the
sabretooth tiger's leaps. Now I couldn't escape it.
So I jumped.

Gia Rose Patel (8)
Burford School, Marlow Bottom

The Great Fire Of London

352 years ago, Thomas Farriner was baking in his bakery and once he had put the bread in the over he went to bed. Then, whilst Thomas was sleeping, the oven shot out tiny sparks of fire. In just a few seconds the bakery was on fire. Thomas woke to crackling flames in front of him. He jumped immediately out the window to safety but when he did he realised his town was also on fire. He ran to the docks and jumped on to a boat and had a lucky escape from London.

Sophie Spicer (8)
Burford School, Marlow Bottom

Mummies Invade

One day, a little girl was born. Her name was Kat because she loved cats and was allergic to dogs. One day she saw something odd, it was slowly approaching on her. She called for her mum and her mum replied in a slow voice, "I'm outside the door." Then Kat knew who the stranger was. It was her mummy who had been turned into a mummy! She opened the door and the mummy came in. Kat got a sword and chopped her head off. That was it, it died.

Ella Rose Parkes (8)
Burford School, Marlow Bottom

The Mystery Monster

In the unilluminated, misty, smoky night, the meek, delightful, enthusiastic girl was walking on the dusty, grubby, ancient bridge when she heard a shriek. At first, she thought it was a feline, then the frightening roar got louder and louder. The scared girl deafeningly screamed, "Help!" as she ran as quickly as a cheetah. Suddenly, the horrific roar stopped. The girl was relieved. She steadily gazed around the city and found a menacing, monstrous, fearsome creature which had a razor-sharp uneven tail and an iridescent skin. What could this bygone, dangerous creature be? A dinosaur!

Mrithika Dhoyamoy Dhar (9)
Falconhurst School, Eaglestone

Trouble With Time Travelling

While travelling through time with my time watch I was thrilled to find a cave full of sheep. Suddenly I heard a giant roar. A Cyclops appeared and said, "I'm going to eat you!"
I was terrified!
"Watch out!" shouted somebody. It was Odysseus, he came to rescue me. As we escaped from the cave, I heard the most beautiful sound like singing. It was sirens, they looked like mermaids but evil. I was lucky as I read about sirens, so I shouted to Odysseus, "Stuff your ears!" and we escaped.
After that, I continued my travel in time.

Erika Plescan (8)
Falconhurst School, Eaglestone

The Heroic Adventure Of Bob

Under the infernal reign of the cretaceous sun, a baby T-rex named Bob questioned himself about where his mother might be. In the end, he explored the small jungle in the corner. As he shot through the vast plants, the smell of a freshly-killed protoceratops filled the air.

All of a sudden, Bob felt hungry. He followed the scent but it led him to two ferocious majungasaurs! He dashed through the dense trees and got lost! He was doomed! But out of nowhere came a weapon called a timeblade. He bit it and a spiral of lightning engulfed him!

Ibraheem Chaudhry (11)
Falconhurst School, Eaglestone

The Creepy Egypt

Once upon a time, there was a boy and his mum. They both went to Egypt because they were bored. Then, all of a sudden, his mum's phone started to ring. The boy was excited and didn't wait for his mum. She was talking on the phone so he went off and walked. When he came back to the place, his mum wasn't there and he felt people surrounding him... There was a zombie mummy monster! But it was kind and it could speak too. It helped the little lost boy find his mum.

Madhushini Thayaparan (9)
Falconhurst School, Eaglestone

The Gods Debate

A long time ago in ancient Greece, there were four gods: Athena, Hermes, Zeus and Poseidon. They were having lunch together discussing their talents.

"My talent is the most useful," said Athena, "So I'm the best god!"

"No! I'm the ruler of the gods," said Zeus.

"It's me," said Hermes.

They argued until Athena said, "Settle down! The people of Greece could use a bar chart to vote."

They met the following Sunday.

"Who won?" asked Hermes.

"We all got twenty-five-per-cent. We're equal," said Athena.

"What a fuss," said Poseidon. So, it turns out all gods are equal and important.

Ajlinka Pinder (10)

Fulbrook Middle School, Woburn Sands

Stone Age Dinner

Wrapped in velvety fur, the Stone Age family closely huddled around the fire keeping cosy and cooking the dodo they'd caught for dinner. To their astonishment, they turned to see a hulking sabre-toothed tiger slickly prowling into their cave, looking for its prey. In a blink of an eye, it sprinted, pouncing for the dodo, taking it rapidly in one swoop into the wilderness to devour. The family collectively breathed a massive sigh of relief, grateful for once to have nothing to eat as it could've easily been one of them who'd ended up as dinner for the tiger.

Sophia Blair (10)
Fulbrook Middle School, Woburn Sands

Wolves

It was midday and everyone was working. We were on watch, we saw some wolves. *Pitter patter*. They scurried over the hill. We ran as fast as we could down to the main hut and told the chief our threat. *Peep* went the chief's shiny metal whistle as he instructed the men to fight. *Clatter, clatter* went the swords as the men prepared for battle. They all looked strong and confident. Nearer came the beasts. All of the children hid with the pigs as the men fought the wolves. Away they ran, however many were killed and father was injured.

Katherine Sinnott (10)
Fulbrook Middle School, Woburn Sands

The Search For The Germans On D-Day

Hundreds of boats crammed with soldiers appear on the horizon in part of the biggest invasion on Europe. Jack is one of the millions who signed up for war, resulting in this mass invasion battling through the German front line. Avoiding shellfire and mines, Jack and his comrades land on the beach and somehow manage to regroup and depart. After days of marching and driving, he starts to become hungry and thirsty because of lack of supplies. However, finally, they find the Nazis. What was about to happen would change his life and the course of the war forever...

Aidan Harris (11)
Fulbrook Middle School, Woburn Sands

The War

He said, "Attack!" So they raised their swords and ran. *Clang! Clang!* went the swords. "Argh!" screamed the Anglo-Saxons. It wasn't a nice view, blood spurting on the battlefield.

There was one Viking who stayed in their hut (which was broken with bricks falling out). He was writing in his diary with a quill on the side. However, he was the son of a great warrior. His name was Ranji. His dad wouldn't let him join in because he was too young. He was seven. But he snuck out of the hut and ran away to the dangerous war.

Aiden Kinns (10)
Fulbrook Middle School, Woburn Sands

The Egyptian Family

Many moons ago there lived a beautiful queen named Cleopatra. One day when she was outside her castle she met the most handsome warrior, aka Julius Caesar. She immediately fell in love. He too liked the queen and from then on they had undeniable love for one another.

Back at the castle, her courtiers were in awe. She had married Caesar and the family began to multiply as they had their three sons and one daughter. Cleo thought she was the luckiest woman in the world. The four children had their own camels and the family lived happily ever after!

Katie E Purdie (10)
Fulbrook Middle School, Woburn Sands

The Forgotten Victims

Bang! The sound of the Titanic splitting in two was deafening. I immediately thought of the delicious eggs in the cargo room spilling into the vast ocean. I rushed to the railings and simply jumped. I landed in the freezing water with a splash. I desperately kicked all of my four paws in the water. Eventually, I reached an iceberg. I saw the Titanic bearing down on the sea as if it was a Big Mac that it was about to devour.

I waited for rescue, and I am still waiting on that iceberg. Forgotten, but very much alive.

Jack Edward Pearson (10)
Fulbrook Middle School, Woburn Sands

Lost In The Crowds

And there I was, in the bustling streets of
Edwardian London in the cobbled market square.
How I had got there I didn't know, but there had to
be a way out. In front of me were grand ladies in
beautiful dresses, and men in tailored suits.
Carriages and carts were all around me, and there
were boys selling sweets and fruits.
Later I saw a group of stunning women in the road
yelling, "We have rights!" Suddenly I realised who
they were! The suffragettes. A policeman came to
get them. Wait a moment... Oh no! He had me too!

Eliza Bennett (10)
Fulbrook Middle School, Woburn Sands

The Nightmare Men

I sprinted across the battlefield. The danger of being caught seemed indescribable. I froze. I already knew who they were. Hearing gunshots at every moment, hearing footsteps coming closer every second. The only words spoken were the whispers of German soldiers, aiming their rifles in every direction, shouting in their foreign language. I huddled in my hiding spot and wished this war would stop. I heard footsteps coming towards me. My heart was pumping as fast as it could... They had found me, but now I knew this woeful war was endless.

Tora Doyle (10)
Fulbrook Middle School, Woburn Sands

Grace O'Malley

I met Grace O'Malley, a pirate. She hadn't always been a pirate. First Grace had to prove to her dad that she was worthy of being a sailor so she wore boys' clothes and cut her hair. He finally let her sail but if they met a pirate ship she had to hide. But she didn't. She jumped out and won the first battle easily. Sailing was not enough though so she became a successful pirate. When the English took her sons, she came to England and formed a surprising friendship with Elizabeth first and then defeated the Spanish army.

Hannah Kincaid (10)
Fulbrook Middle School, Woburn Sands

A Close Shave

A bullet whistled past my ear. *Phew! That was close*, I thought to myself. I peered around the barrel I was hiding behind. As sheriff of this wild, wild town, it was my job to keep the townsfolk safe from outlaws and bandits. Another bullet punctured the barrel and water started to pool at my feet. I ran for cover behind the jailhouse wall. Out of breath, I checked my pistol. A single bullet left. I stepped out into the open, my arm held straight, and fired. The man collapsed to the ground. Billy the Kid was dead!

Ollie Ditty (10)
Fulbrook Middle School, Woburn Sands

Help Me

There I was, held captive in an underground German bunker. I could hear bombs all around me, screams, shouts, leaders screaming, "Move!" I was so scared. I opened my eyes to see a bright light shining in my eyes. Someone was pointing a torch in my face. One of the leaders screamed, "Bring her as well!" I knew he meant me.
I was dragged to a truck. There I was put in a sack. I shut my eyes and expected the worst. Bombs were dropping, people were screaming and all I could do was lie and listen. Please help me!

Eva Cookham (10)
Fulbrook Middle School, Woburn Sands

Mammoth Rampage

It was a sunny, breezy day and a Stone Age man was out hunting for food. Suddenly, the ground began to shake and the trees started swaying to and fro. Then out of the trees appeared a great woolly mammoth. Its tusks were sharp. The man started to run but the mammoth chased after him. They were running for quite a while but then the man turned on the mammoth and even though he didn't want to, he stabbed the mammoth in the heart.

Later, the man and his tribe were sitting around the warm fire eating mammoth stew. Delicious.

Isla Cosby-Ferguson (10)
Fulbrook Middle School, Woburn Sands

Fire, Fire Everywhere

The houses were tumbling down, red-hot flames all around me, nowhere to run. My heart pounding with panic, I'd never seen anything like it. Fire up high, fire down low. I wanted it to stop. We all did. I felt like I was in a flaming oven on 200 degrees. My face turning red. Heat was taking over. This was the end, this was the place that would never survive, this was the place where nobody would be alive. This was the place where bells would no longer ring, because this very unfortunately was... the Great Fire of London.

Gracie Jackson-Krkoska (10)
Fulbrook Middle School, Woburn Sands

Bombs Are Dropping

We were at war and bombs had been dropping for what seemed like forever. I had been playing with my brother when suddenly the air-raid siren went off. We ran with my mother to the underground train station. Lots of people were already there. We sat down and I felt terrified because I could die. Everyone sat in silence until an old man in the corner started singing and soon everyone had joined in. Soon I forgot all about my worries because everyone was having so much fun and time flew by.
Soon we were out. I was alive!

Imogen Charlotte Wright (10)
Fulbrook Middle School, Woburn Sands

Chariot Race

When Augustus was lining up ready for his race, he felt really nervous because it was his first time racing and he didn't want to make his parents angry. As he was lining up he could feel his heart beating. When the whistle went, it was Augustus' time to shine. His horse was galloping down the track. The finish line was in sight for Augustus and he looked behind him and said, "They are not going to catch me."

Augustus galloped over the finish line. He was smiling with joy because he won the race.

Lily-Mae Hartley (10)
Fulbrook Middle School, Woburn Sands

The Great Fire Of London

Lucy and Ben went to the bakery and they smelt smoke. Ben said, "Fire! Fire!" The fire was so strong, smoke filled the streets of London. The fire started on 2nd September and raged over five days. the fire destroyed St Paul's Cathedral and all the wooden buildings in the city. Lucy and Ben and loads of other people ran to the River Thames to flee the raging fire. They had a boat that they stayed on for five days, floating on the Thames until it was safe to return home. Lucy and Ben were glad to be safe.

Ellie Bown (10)
Fulbrook Middle School, Woburn Sands

Mummies

There was a muffled groaning noise coming from behind me. I turned around and I found myself staring into its hole-like eyes. It was a mummy! I thought I would scream but no sound came out. Then it gave chase. There were rooms leading into rooms and we kept going in circles. Soon the mummy trapped me in a room. There was no escape.
But, for some reason, before it got me it groaned again and before I knew it the room was swarming with mummies, all breathing on me, all around me, all trying to kill me...

Henry Kent (10)
Fulbrook Middle School, Woburn Sands

The Mummy

I stood there, bored. I wanted to run away but I couldn't. Then I did. I ran into the ancient pyramid. I knew I shouldn't have done that for the tour guide would've been angry at me! But I did anyway. I ran up millions of stairs, each stair crumbling beneath my feet. I stumbled. I saw a coffin. I was terrified. Slowly the door started to creak open and I saw bundles of toilet paper (or at least it looked like it). No! I was wrong! It was a mummy. I screamed. It was petrifying. I ran away, scared.

Heidi Rose Yems (9)
Fulbrook Middle School, Woburn Sands

The Gods Intervene

In a place called Egypt, there was a queen named Cleopatra. As she watched the bloody war against the Romans, something historical happened. The Greek gods had come to save history. Zeus, Athena, Apollo, Poseidon and Hermes had come to make peace. But it wasn't easy. Since Athena was the goddess of war, she could easily help but then the Roman leader started to mock the gods, even Cleopatra. The gods were fed up with them so they cursed the tribes with the plague for eternity because of their cruelty.

Paris Connor (10)
Fulbrook Middle School, Woburn Sands

The Dragon's Cave

There was a hill. On top of the hill sat a cave with leaves creeping around the rocky floor. Nobody dared go near the cave but one scary night as trees rustled in the howling wind, a boy climbed up that hill. What he saw made him scream so much it felt like his throat was on fire. He was starting to regret his decision. It was the sort of thing he had nightmares about. He tried to run but fear stopped him. He froze in the darkness and as the moonlight appeared, he saw clearly it was a dragon!

Amelia Nicholls (10)
Fulbrook Middle School, Woburn Sands

The Tomb

My name is Thomas Longstaffe and I have never felt so scared in my life. I am running extremely fast through a long tunnel in a tomb. Something is chasing me but I don't want to look back, otherwise, I will fall over and injure myself. In front of me is a corridor of traps, such as crocodile pits, arrows coming out of the walls, bottomless pits and rope swings. I make it to the end of all of them. I trip over and staring me in the eye is an ugly, rotten mummy. I scream. "Argh!"

Thomas Longstaffe (10)
Fulbrook Middle School, Woburn Sands

Being Chased By A Mummy

This may seem odd, but once I was walking along a very strange street when all of sudden an ancient mummy started chasing me. I started running but I thought what might happen if I stopped. I just stopped. She had quite a high-pitched voice and she asked me a very strange question. The question was, "Will you be my friend?"
"Yes, I guess so."
Then she reached her hand over to mine and we walked and walked. Then I said I wanted to go home, so I did.

Millie Wardley (10)
Fulbrook Middle School, Woburn Sands

Cannibals

I was sprinting as fast as I could in a flat area with tall grass. Yelling and muttering behind me and a soft rustle of grass on my ankles. Dogs barking and wolves too. I took a swift look behind me, these men were wearing the skins of dead animals and had clubs with spikes coming out of them. I sped up. The wolves' teeth were watering with hunger. I checked my mind if I'd ever seen or heard men like this who were cannibals. All of a sudden it hit me, they were cavemen!

Alejandro López (9)
Fulbrook Middle School, Woburn Sands

Across The Ocean

My tummy rumbles. It has been two days since I had food. We're on a longboat and I don't think we've been here before as the stars usually show us the way. The captain is going to be cross if we're going the wrong way! It's time for Blacky to go to work. I keep her in a cage and feed her bits of food I save. I'm on the deck and I get Blacky the raven out. "Off you fly Blacky! Find us land, find us food - I'm starving!"

Jake Bradshaw
Fulbrook Middle School, Woburn Sands

Strong Foot

"It seems like the British have taken over." I started running like Sonic. There they were, 20,000 troops. I knew this was going to happen. At the speed of sound, I ran to what I was making (a potion). I took one drop. *Splash!* I was as strong as the Hulk, so when the British came, all it took was one kick from me to shoot the soldiers to outer space. After that, they all started running away.

Alexander Lee (10)
Fulbrook Middle School, Woburn Sands

The Roman Drought

In the harsh years of Rome, Caesar was in his palace until he heard a noise out of his crooked window. People were raging for water.

"We want water!" shouted the people.

Caesar was angry, thinking to himself. As he was going downstairs, he met his servant. Her name was Sara. She was there to tell him something.

"Gandalf has stolen our water!" exclaimed Sara.

"We will execute him!" shouted Caesar.

Off they went to go to Gandalf. He was eating soup.

"Stop!" shouted Caesar.

He was arrested and executed and peace fell over all the land.

Jabir
Priory Primary School, Greyfriars

The Mummy

Once, in Egypt, there were two people, Horenhop and Kamos. They were roaming inside the big pyramid. Kamos leaned on a tile. Immediately, they found a door in front of them!

There was a mummy. Horenhop said, "Run away!" They went to Ahmose, the pharaoh. They told him the story. He said, "I will help you!"

When they went to the pyramid, they didn't find the mummy but then the mummy came back. Kamos was so scared!

Ahmose said, "Throw the water on the mummy!" but the mommy did not die then they shot the mummy, and they killed it.

Moaaz Mostafa Negmeldin (10)
Priory Primary School, Greyfriars

The Fight To Be King

In beautiful London, there lived King Edward. Twenty-five years ruling, it was peaceful but dark clouds invaded. A fight began. "Edward, stand down or fight!" yelled Edward's arch-enemy, Charles.

"Never, you rascal!" yelled back King Edward.

"Then it's war!" demanded Charles.

King Edward went to get his sword and went outside. A gunshot was heard. King Edward and Charles went to war. It was horrible to see. Charles had a cut on the leg. He was injured. Finally, King Edward had his chance and killed Charles. A celebration started for his win but Edward fell to the ground, dead!

Wahid Choudhury (10)
Putnoe Primary School, Bedford

The Mighty Axe

All the gruesome, horrific Vikings were walking through the lovely village that was known as the Anglo-Saxon village, but now was known as the Viking village. Then a boom occurred. The Anglo-Saxons wanted their land back. The Vikings got their axes and shields and ran towards the Anglo-Saxons. There were chopped off heads covered in red, cherry-coloured blood.

The leader of the Saxons was Alfred, he wanted to take on the Viking leader who was Edward. Alfred ran up to Edward, but Edward got his axe and cut his head off with a massive swing. "Alfred's dead!"

Abigail Winn (10)
Putnoe Primary School, Bedford

The Day Of My End

Bang! Another bullet has just shot over my head. Every day is painful, I'm exhausted and lonely. My friend got sent home as he got a Blighty.

I've been thinking, should I get a Blighty? *Bang! Bang! Bang!* "Get down!" I see a big flash of light and *boom!* We had hit a German. We were celebrating.

Many hours later it is my free time so I play cards with the last two friends I have. It isn't good though. It has started to rain. My heart is skipping beats. Before I know it... *Bang!* I am gone.

Shanay Francois (9)
Putnoe Primary School, Bedford

Ancient Actors

Cleopatra died on 12th August 30BC and it all happened like this...
Cleopatra loved Julius Caesar. So when the Romans came to invade, Julius Caesar tried to protect Cleopatra, but Caesar got murdered after they left. So obviously Cleopatra had to love another man but she couldn't choose between Augustus and Mark Antony. She decided to love Mark Antony. When he lost in war against Augustus, Cleopatra was finished. Antony heard that Cleopatra killed herself. He was so upset he decided to kill himself but he failed. Then he heard she was alive!

Numa Nazahah (10)
Putnoe Primary School, Bedford

The Adventure Of WWII

The war was going to happen. Everyone was ready. I climbed into my Blackbird and switched the engine on. *Boom!* A pistol had told us the war had begun. The engines of the planes were revving and roaring. It was time for take-off. As I took off, there were already German planes falling down. My friends were flying beside me in a V-shaped formation. I aimed for a German plane flying in front of me. *Boom!* I shot it down. Then, to my right, came a whole army of German planes. They started shooting everywhere. My beloved plane crashed...

Arjun Sikand (10)
Putnoe Primary School, Bedford

The Sinking Of The Titanic

I was silently sitting on the large ship with my mother and father. Suddenly, the ship crashed into something ahead. I was rapidly blown off my feet. I scrambled back up. That was when I realised that our ship was sinking. Everything happened at once. "Go!" my father yelled at me. The lifeboat was floating outside on the cold ocean. The lifeguard came to the ship and lifted me up onto the lifeboat, along with my mother. *Where is Father?* I thought. Then a few minutes later, someone tapped me on the back. I turned around...

Daniella Adjei-Asante (10)
Putnoe Primary School, Bedford

The First Steps

I was flying my aeroplane when I swirled through a small, slightly black circle in the sky. Before I knew it, I had crash-landed into the unknown. Cautiously, I climbed out of the aeroplane aware of what would come next. I was shocked by what I saw, it was like a jungle! There were vines and trees everywhere. I definitely wasn't home, I didn't know where I was. I started to explore around me. I found a very odd creature in a nest. It was actually quite cute. Suddenly, I heard stomping. My heart pounded with it. A terrifying dinosaur...

Alyssia Brown (10)
Putnoe Primary School, Bedford

World War I

On a cold day in the dreadful trenches, the sloppy mud was in my shivering toes which had blood dripping like a fast, red Ferrari. I was hearing gunshots that went as fast as a millisecond. Luckily, I didn't get shot. After a while, I had no toes because of stupid trench foot. While I was eating my dry, unpleasant rice, I heard footsteps as loud as my heart beating during that moment. It was a filthy rat crawling its little paws around.
Boom! I got shot like a toothpick getting snapped out of nowhere. "Arghhhhh!"

Karan Mahey (9)
Putnoe Primary School, Bedford

Spartans And Winged Hussars

"Spartans! Let's move to the fight till death". I could hear the clattering of the Spartans. We would fight until we died. The shine of my spear, the blood on my sword, the speed of my horse, all gave me confidence for the battle. The shine of my shield, the bang of my heart, the strength of my armour, all gave me spirit to fight. The encouraging shouts of warriors for the battle. My spear was sawing a Spartan's armour. My sword cut a horse's leg. The crashing of an ancient head and helmet as my horse walked over him.

Alexander Buczkowski (10)
Putnoe Primary School, Bedford

Dear Diary Of Cambridge Of WWII

Hello, my name is Penelope and I sometimes feel like I'm the only one alive while sitting on this humungous, fresh field writing on a scrap piece of paper. It's only 1943 and I'm still here with my evacuation family. It's not the worst living here, it just gets dark sometimes. I can hear children running out of their homes. Quietly, birds sing as the river beside swims peacefully. I delightfully smell delicious dinner. I pray and hope to not be blown up or hit by Germany... but I guess it already happened last night...

Gabriela Stryjewska (11)
Putnoe Primary School, Bedford

Miss Unsinkable Violet Jessop

Me, Miss Unsinkable, which is not actually my real name, it's actually Violet Jessop. I was on the Titanic and, at once, I heard a thud. *Crash! Boom!* Everyone was screaming shouting, "Argh! Help me I'm dying!"
They ordered me to go to the top deck to help non-English passengers. I spoke Spanish, French and many more languages. By that time, I was an ocean liner stewardess. Everyone was screaming. They told me to board lifeboat number seventeen. Finally, I was saved. I'd survived an accident at sea.

Delia Florentina Crimu (9)
Putnoe Primary School, Bedford

The Trenches

We were entering the trenches when we heard shots of rifles and men screaming, "Men, dead ahead!" As I looked over to the right, I saw the dead, wretched bodies of my friends. I was mad, very mad. I was so infuriated that I lobbed my grenade over the barbed wire, climbed out of the trench and started firing. After what felt like hours, my gun stopped firing. All of my bullets were gone! I was getting shot at too now. Although I was out of bullets, I kept pushing forward. "Argh!" I was shot in my left shoulder...

Archie Schaffer (10)
Putnoe Primary School, Bedford

Vikings Attack Britain

Whilst I was raying there was a loud bang outside the monastery. When I opened the big wooden door, suddenly smoke and fire were everywhere. Bearded men with swords and axes were killing other monks so I ran to my little straw hut quickly, only to see that all of my precious jewels had been taken. So I ran as fast as I could and grabbed the remains of my belongings.

"Aaargh!" Shouting was right behind me, then I realised a bearded man was chasing me. Suddenly I fell. The man swung his mighty sword and it went black.

Scarlett Smith (10)
Putnoe Primary School, Bedford

Dora And The Dinosaur

I was amazed as I looked at the scaly, humungous beasts with razor-sharp teeth. I tried to get closer but I accidentally slipped and fell into the bushes, which made a loud rustle. My heart started to race. *What if they heard me?* I thought, while scrambling to my feet.

Roar! I quickly jumped to my feet and ran. I could hear my heart beating loudly, along with loud thumps on the ground. I ran like my life depended on it. What could happen now? What if I died? I hoped I'd get to see my friends again...

Leana Tihomirova (9)
Putnoe Primary School, Bedford

The Challenge

I was standing inside the Epsom Derby in 1913, the adrenaline rushing through my veins and my heart pounding with great fear like I had never felt before. As the horses thundered around the corner, I sprinted towards the king's horse. As I got closer the horses went faster and time slowed down. I stretched out my arms and tumbled to the ground. I could faintly see the hooves of the horse galloping all over me. The last thing I remembered was my eyes closing and the shouts and screams of the people fading into silence...

Alaia Elizabeth Walton-Kale (11)
Putnoe Primary School, Bedford

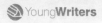

World War II Sacrifice

Bang! All I could hear was the *rat-tat* of rain on my plane. The boom of shots being fired. I was terrified. As my plane soared through the sky, I looked around. Pilots were drowning and burning up. I fired my bomb on an enemy plane. *Boom!* As I turned my plane around I saw it, a German Hurricane. I gulped, my heart started to race. I fired a shot but the pilot dodged it just in time. My heart went even quicker, my breathing as well. A bomb came towards me but I didn't have time to dodge it.

Georgia Coblenz (9)
Putnoe Primary School, Bedford

The Dinosaur Hunt

The trees bowed to the wind and the ground shook. I grabbed my knife, though I knew it wouldn't be enough. The huge monster growled and its bloodstained fangs were bared. I charged the creature as it loomed over me. It reared its ugly head. I slid under it and grabbed the tail as it flicked it up while its head crashed into the ground. Panic clawed at my chest as I flipped ungracefully off the tail onto the head. I grabbed its jaws and the dinosaur flicked its head, sending me flying. It charged at me as I fell...

George Mhitaryan (10)
Putnoe Primary School, Bedford

The Truce

I felt as if I could hear someone singing carols. Was it the end of the war? I didn't know. Suddenly the German leader stepped onto no-man's-land, then the British leader joined him. They had a small conversation but no one could hear. Then the German leader pulled out a ball from his jacket. A football match started. Suddenly more and more people joined. Others were exchanging gifts, food and drink and playing cards until *bang! Bang! Crash!* The war was back on and nobody could do anything about it.

Ibrahim Ali Hussain (10)
Putnoe Primary School, Bedford

118

The First Day Of War

I was breathing heavily, my heart pounding, beating at 200bpm. I leapt as far as I could, then I heard a deafening *boom!* My life flashed before my eyes several times. My childhood, my short adulthood, everything! I heard ringing in my ears, then I closed my eyes. I wanted it to stop. I lay there, grabbing anything I could to get up and run. I used my gun to get myself up, and I'd just started running when they started to shoot. I felt the heat as a bullet zoomed past my ear when I suddenly collapsed...

Michael Oliver (10)
Putnoe Primary School, Bedford

The Beast

I, Max Jones, am on an expedition through time. In the jungle, I see the long-dormant volcano which is about to explode. There I see a hut made of straw and wood. Inside is a man named Bill on the hunt for dinosaurs and there it is, a T-rex damaged and weak, like something attacked it, something bigger and stronger. I think to myself what could have happened to a T-rex of that size? Then I hear a growl louder than the T-rex. I see footprints the size of me. Oh my gosh, there it is. The beast...

Dane Robertshaw (10)
Putnoe Primary School, Bedford

The First Flight

I ran and ran to my Spitfire. My heart was going *bam! Boom!* Once in the dark, cloudy sky, I was full of fear. What was going to happen to me? I could hear the whiz of my engine and the bangs of huge roaring guns. Even the tip tap of the rain made me jump. Behind me, I could see the other soldiers in their wrecked Spitfires. I was so frightened, was I even going to see my family again? I wanted to go slower and turn back; I couldn't though. Then I saw the fighting Germans...

Isabelle Smith (9)
Putnoe Primary School, Bedford

The Lost Tomb Of Tutankhamun

I was walking in quieter than a mouse. It was dark and quiet. I turned on my flashlight and saw something unbelievable. The tomb of Tutankhamun! I carefully opened it. For a split second, I thought I was hallucinating but I wasn't. It was true, he was alive! He chased after me, quicker than a cheetah. Then... everything went dark. I was trapped. All I could hear was the tip tap of Tutankhamun's footsteps as he returned to his tomb. Then it all went silent. Everything was lost.

Amelia Kulik (10)
Putnoe Primary School, Bedford

The Mummy

The soft sand fell. A lever appeared near the door so she pulled it. A loud rumbling sound shook the floor and the door opened. She walked in and found a gold tomb. "Um hello?" said the girl. She opened the dusty, golden tomb and saw a mummy. There was a table of bottles with mysterious liquids in them, she picked one up and poured a drop on her finger. Nothing happened. So she poured it on the mummy then it blinked. The girl pounced back, but the mummy saw her. It got up...

Faith Flawn (10)
Putnoe Primary School, Bedford

Tutankhamun

I ran and ran until I ran out of breath. I couldn't believe I'd let a grave robber trick me into stealing the mummy's goods. As I caught my breath, I realised that I had just awoken Tutankhamun. This was not going to end well. As I stepped back, I fell on the golden sand. By the time I got up, everyone was gone. The mummy got closer. So I scrambled up onto my feet and "Argh!" I was dragged into the mummy's bloody lair, unable to escape...

Niamh Bailey (10)
Putnoe Primary School, Bedford

Vikings Invading Britain

My king demanded I and one million other Vikings onto a ship to attack Scotland. So I rowed for hours a day and it took us five long days. When we got there, we didn't kill one person, we killed every one of them so we could take over the land, and made sure no one was left. If we saw anyone we would blow them up and make a house. As we made our way down the country, we killed more people, ready for the blazing hot fire for that night.

Jack Garratt (9)
Putnoe Primary School, Bedford

The Day I Was At War

I saw all of my fellow comrades die right in front of my blue, gem-like eyes. One of the German fighters was running at me. I couldn't see who he was but I ran, screaming loudly, shooting madly. My heart was pounding like a wild cheetah growling. "Hey! Who are you?" shouted the German fighter. I didn't say anything. Would anyone save me now? Why did I decide to get into this?

Jessica Jayne Hawkins (10)
Putnoe Primary School, Bedford

The Midnight Mummy

Lightning struck the abandoned pyramid and the old Egyptian mummy arose from its deathly trance. He had decaying bandages and was murmuring, "Help me!" in a faint voice. It appeared that he was hurt as he stumbled towards me. I was only there to see my uncle's grave.

It stopped dead in its tracks about three metres away from me. Then it said in a voice that I vaguely remembered, "Come here!"

My blood ran cold. I ran back home, terrified, the dreadful scene still in my head. Suddenly, I realised something important; that mummy I saw, was my uncle...

Ethan Andrew Rushton (8)
Sharnbrook Primary School, Sharnbrook

The Vikings

The chief was shaking his fist, making his cheeks red. The chief blew his horn so the smith came rushing to him. As he came to the chief, the smith felt nervous because he was growling louder and louder. "Make me some chainmail!" roared the chief.

The smith dashed back to his hut and his friends to make the chief some armour. The smith worked until they had the chief's armour ready. The smith returned to the chief and gave him his armour. The smith continued working on the swords and shields so all the fighters were ready for battle.

Ezequiel Cutting (9)
Sharnbrook Primary School, Sharnbrook

The Egyptian Adventure

Once there was a young boy called Jake. He loved Egyptians. He took a shortcut home from school and saw a weird-looking man who was a time traveller. Jake said, "Excuse me, but can you take me to Egyptian times?"
The time traveller said, "Yes of course!"
He went in the time machine and, in seconds, he was in Egyptian times. He stepped out of the time machine and into a huge pyramid, but then he bumped into the Queen and a mummy! The Queen shouted, "Get that boy!" Jake ran to the time machine and got home safely.

Storm Chambers (8)
Sharnbrook Primary School, Sharnbrook

George Washington's Life Journey 1732-1799

George was born in 1732. In his childhood, he moved house several times within three years. Sadly his grandfather died when he was eleven. Imagine only knowing your grandparents for eleven years - how would you feel?

At eleven years of age, he had ten slaves and also had wooden teeth.

By seventeen he owned his first horse.

In 1776 when England ruled America, Americans were forced to drink tea but George made a gang and threw it all in the sea. That helped him to be the first president. He died in 1799.

Harrison Michael Welch (9)
Sharnbrook Primary School, Sharnbrook

Viking Adventure

Lizzie could time travel. One day, she decided to time travel back to the Vikings. she found herself in Scandinavia, next to a house. She walked in and met Gazelda who was sad because she couldn't work on the farm. Instead, she cooked, cleaned and washed. Her dad Garof was going to set off for war. They decided to convince her parents to let her work on the farm. Lizzie drew posters for Grazelda. Her parents decided she could work on the farm! Garof made a ring for Lizzie and then she went home.

Jessica Steele (9)
Sharnbrook Primary School, Sharnbrook

The Hugging Mummy!

It was the dead of night. Everyone was watching a person being mummified. I was there too because the person being mummified was my gran! I was devastated.

The next day, I went back. She began to reach out her arms. I sprinted into a field and into a maze. I ran too deep. My heart stopped; I was at a dead-end! What could I do? Where could I go? I was trapped! She approached me. She reached out her arms and pulled me to her chest and... hugged me! Then she returned to her tomb. Good old Gran.

Eloise Hope Cannon (9)
Sharnbrook Primary School, Sharnbrook

The Mummy Chase

One day in Egypt, a detective was searching for an undiscovered tomb. After days of looking, he found it. Then he swept away the door and crept inside... There was a golden statue, jars containing body parts and some leftover bandages. But, when he finally got to the mummies, they were awake! Then they chased him. He was chased out and hid on top of the pyramid. When he was found he played dead. When they went, he ran, but got chased all the way back to England!

Ava Howard (9)
Sharnbrook Primary School, Sharnbrook

Dinosaur Brethren

As Kai, the most cunning voyager, secretively lurked under the cavorting trees, the bleak landscape was engulfed in wild, monstrous predators. Kai deeply hoped not to be discovered by the tyrant, beastly dinosaurs. He thoroughly enjoyed his escapade of tranquilising the dinosaur and retrieving its abnormal blood. As he absent-mindedly strolled through the damp earth, he remembered how beautiful this island was. The land was exotic and mouth-watering with secrets ready to be unlocked. As he turned around, he saw the dinosaur that would almost make your exoskeleton want to run away... the thesaurus!

Darren Kunaishe Machingauta (11)
St Mary's RC Primary School, Caddington

Titanic

One stormy day, the crystal water started to crash loudly against the rocks. As they were on the enormous ship, they jumped with fright. All of the people were panicking and terrified, not knowing what to do. Ashley thought they crashed and then all of a sudden, Lilly came running up to her. "Ashley, we crashed into one of the biggest icebergs ever. I'm so scared and hysterical, I'm about to faint," she said, terrified.

"Lilly, look, the water is coming inside. We need to go and help the people."

Then, all of a sudden, the ship started sinking...

Ashley Claude Sheila Davies (11)
St Mary's RC Primary School, Caddington

Fiercely, Ferociously Fight

One murky, mumbling day, the English soldiers were getting ready for war to start in Belgium. While they were getting ready, the sneaky Germans were roaming around with stress.

One prolonged hour later, the battle began. All of their hearts were beating madly in the silence. The English soldiers were thundering out, "I shall destroy you people!" The guns were blowing with surprise and bombs were attacking many places nearby. Many of the people were hurt and had lost many important body parts.

A couple of years later, England had won the battle. Home they went...

Rosie Ellis-Emery (11)
St Mary's RC Primary School, Caddington

The First World War

I'm Jeffrey and I'll tell the story of the First World War. *Ring!* went the bell for breakfast. I had to wake up and go to the canteen. For breakfast, I had porridge. Then I got dressed to go and attack on the battlefield. My team were hidden so that the opponents couldn't see us. A group of soldiers stepped outside. They saw all of the people on the other side. Then we ferociously shot them.
After one minute, the other countrymen were all lying on the bloody floor - dead. "Hooray!" cheered everyone from our team.

Emma Lawrence (11)
St Mary's RC Primary School, Caddington

Zeus' Revenge

Sprinting through the damp, cold maze, trying to gain back my powers. "Roar!" The Minotaur came running ar me, although it was too late for him as I realised my godly powers had returned. I zoomed back to the thundery, grey cloud home.

The next day, I was ready for revenge, running back to the maze with my lightning staff. I opened the door, dragged the Minotaur out and suffered him with my lightning staff. As it was ripping further and further into his chest, I saw something else come out. It had skin. It was human!

Michal Antoniuk (11)
St Mary's RC Primary School, Caddington

Larry's Mistake

The king found a young man and greeted him by saying, "Salutations my comrade. You look like a fine fellow for my army. Go get ready for battle." But the man called Larry didn't agree with this and told the king to stop immediately. This annoyed the king and that was the biggest mistake of Larry's life The king wasn't pleased with this so he banished him to be locked up in the battle coliseum. He had to hold up the atlas stone with no food or water. Larry always struggled to hold it up.

Sonny Bateman (10)
St Mary's RC Primary School, Caddington

World War Two

Dear diary, today was stressful. Winston Churchill declared war on Germany. I was mortified. I live with my mum, brother and uncle. My uncle is going to serve in the army to help. I am very scared. I don't want him to get hurt. My little brother is only young and he doesn't understand. My mum has been crying all day. I don't have to go to school now but I have to live in a dirty Anderson shelter. The shelter smells like damp, dirty hair. Also, there is dust and mud everywhere. I will really miss my uncle.

Ronnie-Mae Begley (11)
St Mary's RC Primary School, Caddington

Life In The War With Walter Tull

Hello, my name's Walter Tull and I fought in the atrocious WWII. I entered to sign up. I was one of the few black men to fight the war. During the war, I had to go to hospital because I was suffering from shellshock.

After two years, I had recovered and I travelled back to fight. When I had a break, I trained to be a commander. I achieved my goal of being a commander. I led my men across no-man's-land but was shot in the neck with a machine gun bullet. That was the end of me.

Gabriel Darling (10)
St Mary's RC Primary School, Caddington

Cleopatra's Big Opportunity Of Kindness

Queen Cleopatra was having a slumber party at her palace. Next up was the dance battle and, of course, Cleopatra won and Sarah lost by 1879 points. Then it was the mummy pillow fight and Mariam won. Then there was a *bang*. Sarah went crazy as a mummy started throwing hypnotism stones. He said, "If you want to unfreeze her, say these words: 'hocus pocus one, two, three, everybody unfreeze, make us all friends and make me more pretty'."

Cleopatra said them. *Poof!* Everything went back to normal and Cleopatra discovered makeup!

Irisz Ubierbor King (8)
The Linden Academy, Luton

The Celts

One day, Astrid fell into a boat. Heather tried to help but she fell in too. The boat slowly drifted away from shore. They ended up in Rome! A boy was late for school. He ran past Heather and Astrid talking about what they'd do when they got back to Ireland.

"Wait, you're Celts?" said the boy.

"Now he knows we're Celts, let's just take him prisoner," said Astrid. They all got back to Ireland safe and sound.

The next day, Heather and Astrid decided to let the boy go. He decided to join the Celts.

Emily Grace Phinn (8)
The Linden Academy, Luton

World War Two

Years ago, there were two courageous men whose dads sacrificed themselves to save England. Now, it's their turn to sacrifice their bodies. They were in the army so they went into the strongest cargo boat and it was like a house.

The next morning, they arrived in the Australian rainforest. They saw the enemies close by so they hurried up to build their defences. Then Axel and Richard got the RPGs set up, picked up the sniper and with four shots, *bam, wham, boom, pow,* they won. They went home together.

Jonathan Kwaku Henaku Ansah (8)
The Linden Academy, Luton

The Pharaoh

Once upon a time, Mirzi and Cumzi went inside the pyramid. Cumzi went in first. It was so dark. Mirzi went in and fell over. She pushed a button and woke up a pharaoh. Mirzi ran away while Cumzi was exploring the pyramid. She found a button but she was scared to press it after Mirzi pressed the button. Cumzi was scared but pressed the button. She found a pot of gold.
Mirzi hid behind a rock. The pharaoh kept running and Mirzi went back to Cumzi. They took the pot of precious gold and ran. It was heavy.

Ume-Laila Kazmi
The Linden Academy, Luton

Vikings Face A Tarantula

The Viking gods and goddesses returned to protect citizens. They saw exploding dynamite coming from a whole village. Odin flew and Thor carried Freyja, but when they got there they couldn't see the villain because there was a tarantula! With one bite you would die. Thor used his hammer and Odin used his spear and shot it in the sky. Last but not least Freyja used her love. Together they made a purple beam and they defeated the tarantula.

Amerie Njawaya (8)
The Linden Academy, Luton

The Viking And His Dinosaurs

One day, there was a Viking with lots of pets. He lost his dinosaurs and he was very sad. Then he found a fairy. He asked the fairy if she could find his dinosaurs and bring them home to the magical forest. The fairy came back but she didn't find them.

The next day the fairy finally found the dinosaurs. The Viking was so happy he kept them safe forever and ever. He would never let them out of the kingdom again.

Lilie Rosie Gray (8)
The Linden Academy, Luton

The Festival

Fireworks sparked in the midnight sky as the scents of fresh dumplings and sweet caramel apples burst through the air. Suddenly, a stream of flames struck through the lanterns as villagers scattered. Windows slammed, gates shut.
Soon, not even the tiniest mouse was to be seen amongst the cold, empty streets of China. Except one girl. *Click, clack, click, clack.* A pair of little feet scampered through the cowering village. Citizens watched in confusion. A cherry-red firework was lit into the pitch-black sky. In an instant, the dragon fled back into the land above the clouds, never revealing why...

Jin Saleyi (11)
Whitehouse Primary School, Whitehouse

Explosive!

Tumbling mid-air, I gulp hard, trying to understand what just happened. A milky, glimmering pastel of lavender, sapphire-blue and ebony-black dye became a tapestry of jewels and scarves standing tall before me. I sense an icy shiver run down my spine, rapidly spreading through my jittering body. I can't decide what creates it, the dangerous temperature of the new emptiness that forms up my heart. The scene engulfing me is picturesque: I decide I like it here. It's peaceful. Until I hear it. Until I hear the piercing explosion that surely deafens me. A blast. A blare. The Big Bang.

Francesca Charalambous (12)
Whitehouse Primary School, Whitehouse

The Dead King Arises

The tomb. Cold. Dark. Mysterious. Nothing was interesting other than the patterns of the motionless coffin of the powerful. The coffin, that was covered in dust and cobwebs, was enclosed with all the treasure you could ever ask for. Ancient coins from long ago, diamonds and gems scattered everywhere and magic lamps here and there. Plus a bunch of other golden and silver wonders. Tearing the silence, the coffin had a mind of its own as it opened, making a long, slow *creeaaaak!* But the question was, was it the coffin that opened itself, or the soul within...?

Shubh Suman (10)
Whitehouse Primary School, Whitehouse

I Want My Mummy!

As I came back to my senses, I didn't notice my lifeless surroundings until I blinked. A scorching, sandy sensation blew over me. I watched the sun's razor daggers torture me. Two pyramids the size of two million football pitches came into my view while my thoughts toppled over me. I remember my dad giving me two dolls (apparently mummies). I immediately threw them in the bin then found myself here.

Two great figures towered over me. Their mean, snarling faces glancing at me. Both exchanging thoughts of what to do to me. Then, I recognised them...

Loyin Assan (11)
Whitehouse Primary School, Whitehouse

The Pyramid Of Peril

A bead of sweat ran down my forehead. My torch flame flickered around the hieroglyphics. The way out was a trap of snakes and arrows, too hard to see in the dark. In front of the hieroglyphics on the floor was an alternative. Knowing the method was easy: pick the right stone, find what you cherish, pick the wrong stone, truly perish.

I leapt to the first one. Perfect. I took a deep breath as I stepped to the next. Correct. Stepped. Wrong one! I plummeted to the ground as my life flashed before me. Spikes came closer then... darkness.

Hayden Woodall (11)
Whitehouse Primary School, Whitehouse

Its Eyes

At dusk, me and my friends were in the woods, climbing trees together until we heard a thudding noise from the far distance. We all looked at each other in fear. It got louder and louder meaning it got closer and closer. I froze, not knowing what to do. I turned around and looked through the leaves of the trees to see a colossal pair of eyes staring at me. There was a tornado of thoughts and emotions spinning around my confused head. Without thinking, I jumped out of the tree. It grabbed me tight and its jaws opened wide...

Aathmika Kiritharan (11)
Whitehouse Primary School, Whitehouse

Ready

The mild summer breeze rattled a canopy of leaves that towered over me as the jaguar and I fixed eyes. "Roar!" He sharpened his nails; I took my dagger out.

"One, two, three," I said under my breath. He leapt over me; I pushed him and impaled him as quick as possible. I then grabbed the dark, amber fur and swung it on. A parrot with shades of royal blue and cherry red glided down and perched on the tree that I was under. I got the feathers that fell and ran fast. I knew I was ready for pok-ta-pok.

Marta Monteiro (11)
Whitehouse Primary School, Whitehouse

Escaping The Death Of The Dinosaur

In the soundless woods, I sat on a long log until I came face-to-face with my biggest fear. My heart went numb and froze just by looking at his fatal teeth, which might have led to my death. Hunger stood in its eyes. It wanted me...
I started to sprint away from the beast. It followed me; it started to growl at me. Before I knew it, I'd run for miles and miles, hoping to lose my predator. However, it was still behind me with hunger in its teeth. I gave up. I stopped. I looked at the dinosaur...

Jai Nathwani (11)
Whitehouse Primary School, Whitehouse

Harry And It

It was no ordinary woods and Harry walked into it. No animals dared to go here and nobody came out alive ever...

Harry was walking for about an hour and came to a plain. Suddenly, the ground started to shake and he saw an old Jeep left there. He saw a huge pack of gallimimus but who was chasing them? If it was going for them, would it go for him? He ran to the end of the forest, away from everything, until he saw its tail. He thought he knew what it was but he was wrong...

Aadil Khota (11)
Whitehouse Primary School, Whitehouse

YOUNG WRITERS INFORMATION

We hope you have enjoyed reading this book – and that you will continue to in the coming years.

If you're a young writer who enjoys reading and creative writing, or the parent of an enthusiastic poet or story writer, do visit our website www.youngwriters.co.uk. Here you will find free competitions, workshops and games, as well as recommended reads, a poetry glossary and our blog.

If you would like to order further copies of this book, or any of our other titles give us a call or visit **www.youngwriters.co.uk**.

Young Writers
Remus House
Coltsfoot Drive
Peterborough
PE2 9BF

(01733) 890066
info@youngwriters.co.uk

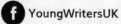 YoungWritersUK

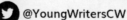 @YoungWritersCW